The Flying Bath

For Felix – J.D.
For Christine Isteed – D.R.

First published 2014 by Macmillan Children's Books
This edition published 2017 by Macmillan Children's Books
an imprint of Pan Macmillan,
20 New Wharf Road, London N1 9RR
Associated companies throughout the world
www.panmacmillan.com

ISBN: 978-1-5098-7891-8

Text copyright © Julia Donaldson 2014
Illustrations copyright © David Roberts 2014
Moral rights asserted.

1 3 5 7 9 8 6 4 2

A CIP catalogue record for this book is available from the British Library.

Printed in China

WRITTEN BY
JULIA DONALDSON

ILLUSTRATED BY
DAVID ROBERTS

The Flying Bath

MACMILLAN CHILDREN'S BOOKS

Wings out, and off we fly.
The Flying Bath is in the sky!

Wings out, and off we fly.

The Flying Bath is in the sky!

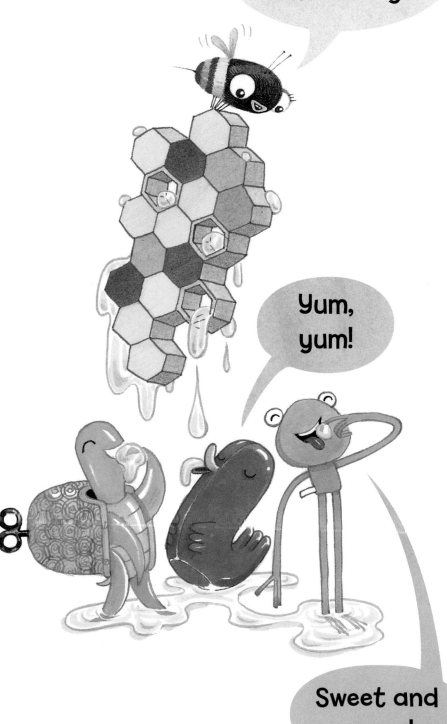

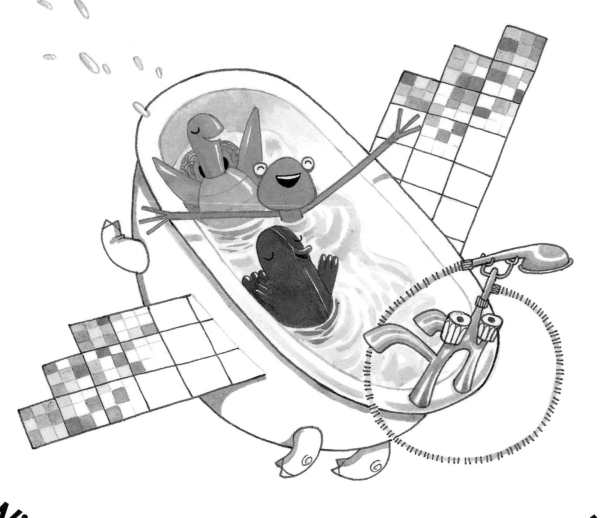

Wings out, and off we fly.
The Flying Bath is in the sky!

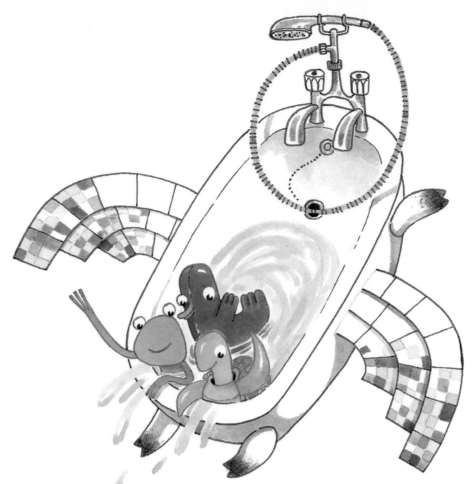

Wings out, and off we fly.
The Flying Bath is in the sky!

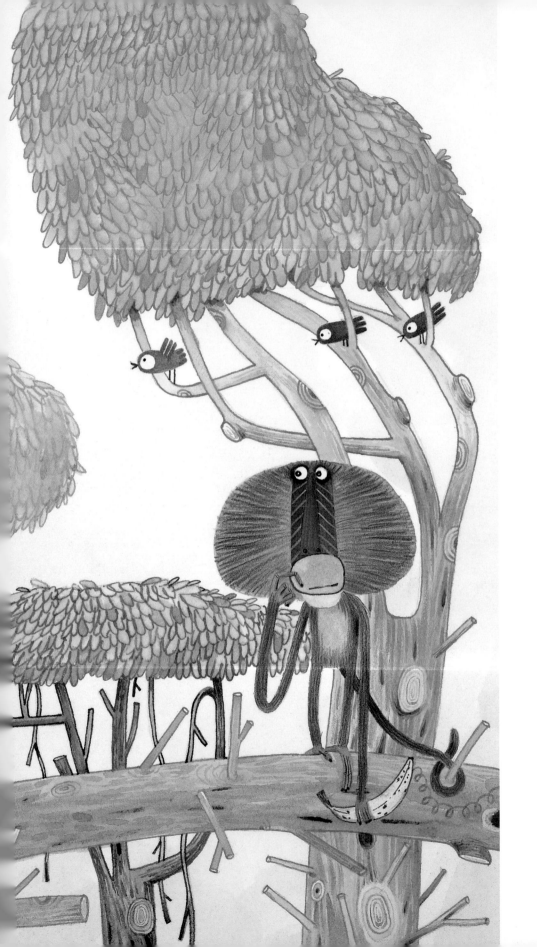

Wings out, and off we fly.
The Flying Bath is in the sky!

. . . but now it's late.
The Flying Bath has got a date.

Wings out, and off we fly.
The Flying Bath is in the sky!